NIGHT FALL

THE PROTECTORS

VAL KARLSSON

MINNEAPOLIS

Text copyright © 2010 by Lerner Publishing Group, Inc.

All rights reserved. International copyright secured. No part of this book may be reproduced, stored in a retrieval system, or transmitted in any form or by any means—electronic, mechanical, photocopying, recording, or otherwise—without the prior written permission of Lerner Publishing Group, Inc., except for the inclusion of brief quotations in an acknowledged review.

Darby Creek
A division of Lerner Publishing Group, Inc.
241 First Avenue North
Minneapolis, MN 55401 U.S.A.

Web site address: www.lernerbooks.com

Cover design: Emily Love
Cover photograph: Photo Words, Inc./iStockphoto

Karlsson, Val.
The protectors / by Val Karlsson.
p.   cm. — (Night fall)
ISBN 978-0-7613-6144-2 (lib. bdg. : alk. paper)
[1. Horror stories.] I. Title.
PZ7.K14248Pr 2010
[Fic]—dc22   2010003317

Manufactured in the United States of America
1—BP—7/15/10

To Jonas P. MacFearson,
dedicated fighter of evil
in this world and beyond!

*Deep into that darkness peering, long I stood there
wondering, fearing,
Doubting, dreaming dreams no mortal ever dared
to dream before*

—*Edgar Allan Poe,* The Raven

1

I'll never forget the day my stepfather locked me in a room full of caskets and left me there for twenty-four full hours. I had no food, nothing to do but lie in casket after casket. Some were cushioned and lined with satin, some lined with velvet, some just plain, hard wood. I lay in each one, imagining what it was like to be dead.

I was ten then. And what did I do to deserve being locked in that room overnight? I don't really know. But then again, my stepfather often got mad at me for no reason at all.

My mom had left that morning for an overnight trip. She often went out to people's homes to do spirit-contact sessions, cleansing ceremonies, things like that. She would hold weird rituals with candles and burning herbs. She would go into a sort of trance. My stepfather hated it.

This was the first time she was going to stay overnight, because of the distance.

"He was in my way, and he was causing trouble," he told my mother after she returned and I had told her what had happened.

"But Sal, you can't just lock a kid up! And with no food!" She hugged me tightly and stroked my hair.

The look he gave me at that moment—I'll never forget it. It made me want to run away forever.

Up until that day, it had been life as usual in a family funeral home. Being in a room full of caskets was nothing new for me, actually. I grew up around coffins, cadavers, embalming tables, scalpels, the laboratory odor of formaldehyde. You see, I lived in a funeral home: Signorelli Funeral Home, my stepfather's family business going back five generations.

I spent hours watching Sal in the mortuary prep room in the basement of our big, old, gray house. I learned the craft of preserving bodies for the funeral display. I observed him draining bodies of all their blood and filling their veins with chemicals. I watched him cut into abdomens and chests with the sharp-pointed trocar to suck out the fluids from their bodies. I watched him pump in a formaldehyde solution. When I was tall enough to reach the embalming table, Sal started to let me help him. "When you're older, Luke, you'll go to school for this and get certified," he'd say. "But you will learn everything you need right here."

I was just nine years old when Dr. Miller died. Sal had me put in the eye caps. That was to prop his eyelids up as his eyeballs started to sink back into their sockets. Then I helped again when our nosy neighbor Mrs. Chase had a heart attack. I held her jaw in place as Sal "shot" a wire in with an injector gun to keep her mouth shut. That was something she *never* did while she was alive. I didn't dare joke about it, though. Sal was always very serious about his work. These were the first of my many hands-on experiences, which got more complex over the next few years.

I would watch Mom work too. She was the cosmetician. That is, she would dress and put makeup on the dead people and fix their hair. She loved doing it. She felt she was giving people a last bit of dignity before they were buried. It was amazing to watch her transform cold, lifeless flesh and make it look warm and living again. That's how Mom was. She could bring life into any room, even an embalming room.

I guess things started getting really weird after

I turned sixteen. That fall I was hanging out with Lincoln and my girlfriend, Aisha, a lot. Lincoln had been my best friend since elementary school. He had a pretty strange family too. Both of his parents were alcoholics. Lincoln's grandfather had died a few years back. He had been a wealthy guy, and now Lincoln's family lived off the money he'd left them. Lincoln lived in a huge house with a pool. But even Lincoln could see that, with his parents' extravagant lifestyle, the money wasn't going to last.

"My mother bought a crystal swan statue on the Internet last night," Lincoln complained one day at lunch. He, Aisha, and I always sat together. Sometimes Lincoln would bring along one of his girlfriends, but today it was just the three of us.

"How much did that cost?" I asked, taking a bite of my ham sandwich.

"Twenty, thirty thousand . . ." Lincoln scowled.

Aisha sucked in her breath. "Geez, how big *is* it?"

"Huge," Lincoln muttered. "I think she was drunk when she ordered it."

"You'd have to be," Aisha said, her dark eyes flashing. "How tacky." Aisha would probably be the last person in the world to purchase a giant crystal swan. She wasn't interested in wealth or material objects. Instead, she focused on the natural world. She knew more about different plants and animals than anyone I'd ever met.

As the three of us walked out of school that afternoon, Aisha tugged at my elbow. "Want to see that movie about whales I was telling you about tonight?" she asked with a smile. "It's showing downtown at eight."

I was always bored during those nature movies, but it would be fun to go with Aisha. We'd both been so busy with school that we hadn't had a real date in a while.

"Sure," I said. "As long as no one dies tonight."

Aisha crossed her fingers for good luck as she

turned to walk down her street. She knew by now that I usually had to help Sal out when a new body was brought in.

But when I got home that night and heard Sal yelling, I knew I wouldn't be going to the movies.

I could hear the trouble before I even entered the house.

"Listen to me!" Sal was yelling. "You're not even listening!"

A part of me wanted to turn around and head to Lincoln's or Aisha's. But I always worried about Mom when Sal was angry. I'd never seen him lay a hand on her. He got so angry, though. I was always worried things could turn violent.

"What about me?" I heard him shout upstairs as I walked into the kitchen. "You're always going off to these people's houses, Penny. What—you're going to talk to Sofia Morelli's dead husband?"

I'd already heard this argument a couple dozen times. It was always the same. Only the names changed. Mom believed she could communicate with the dead. People often contacted her to help them speak with their dead relatives. But Sal was never one to believe in ghosts.

"There's a scientific explanation for everything, Penny," he would say. "A body is a body—all skin, bones, and blood. And nothing more." So every time my mother left for a séance, he got angry.

I actually agreed with Sal about science over spirits. But at the same time, his coldness was depressing. I liked my mother's wacky ideas and warm spirituality. I didn't believe in the stuff, of course. But I have to admit, I preferred her approach to life and death.

"Sal, please," my mother pleaded. "These people need me."

"What about what I need? I need you here. You can't stay here to talk to your own husband, who's alive? Huh?"

"Sal, let me go!"

I heard a door slam and then my mother running down the stairs toward the front door. She saw me sitting in the kitchen. I could see her face fall as she realized that I had heard everything. She came over to me and hugged me. I heard a door open upstairs, then stomping.

"Oh, so you *do* have time for the *boy*, don't you? For the *boy*, of course!" Sal growled as he thundered downstairs.

"Sal, you are being unreasonable. I would give you a hug too, if you'd let me. But I won't come near you when you're like this!" Mom turned and walked out the front door.

"Come with me!" Sal barked at me after the door shut behind my mother. "We have work to do."

We had to embalm two bodies that night—a husband and wife killed in a car accident. Sal put me to work on the husband. I was so nervous from the fight that I spilled embalming chemicals all over the floor when I went to hook up the machine to the husband's carotid artery.

"What have you done?" Sal roared. "Get out of here! You're completely useless!" He grabbed me by the collar and shoved me toward the door.

I called Aisha to let her know that I wouldn't make it to the movie that night. There was no way Sal would let me leave the house.

"That guy is such a jerk. It's so weird, because he's always so nice when I'm around," Aisha said.

"Yeah," I said. "He has a good game face."

"I just don't get why your mom married him."

"That makes two of us," I said.

I got off the phone with Aisha and locked myself in my room so I wouldn't have to deal with

Sal. The longer my mother was away, the more angry he seemed to get.

Sitting alone in my room, hoping Sal wouldn't come barging in, I thought about my Protectors. My mom believed that the spirits of people who died stayed with the last person to handle their bodies. They became that person's "Protectors," she said, "with a capital P." This was an old legend from a small, little-known American Indian tribe called the Mannahassa. It was significant to my mother because she was half Mannahassa. I always thought it was a crazy idea. But when I was afraid or really worried about something, I often found myself thinking about any Protectors I might have.

"You must have a thousand Protectors!" I told my mom one day, joking. She was usually the last one to handle the bodies, both before and after funeral services. She smiled.

"I know I have a few," she replied.

"So, what about people who are murdered and

whose bodies are never found? Do their spirits become the Protectors of the murderers?"

"No," answered Mom, "of course not. When I talk about the last person to handle the body, I mean the last person to *care* for the body. To treat the body with respect and love. To prepare it for a proper burial. If the last person to handle a body has done so with disrespect, or worse, that doesn't count. In fact, that could mean trouble for the person. The spirit will haunt that person."

Later that night, Mom returned from the séance and came to check on me.

"Honey?" I heard her at my door. "Are you okay, Luke?"

"Yeah, Mom. You can come in."

"Is it Sal, hon?"

I didn't say anything, but the look on my face must have.

"You know, Luke, he's had a very lonely life."
She stroked my hair. "I don't think he ever learned
how to show people he cares about them. When he
was a boy, his father was very cruel to him."

That I'd heard before. Sal had grown up in
Bridgewater with his parents and one brother. The
family ran the funeral business back then, too.
Everyone in town still talked about Sal's parents.
His mother would do strange things all the time,
like carry bags of sugar around with her like they
were her babies. She had left the family when Sal
was still quite young. Sal's father, Charlie, had a
reputation for being hot-tempered. They called
him "Crazy Charlie." Eventually, he climbed into an
open coffin, lay back, and slit his own wrists.

Most people got along with Sal. He was cheerful
in town, but grumpy at home. But I'd heard some
people say that, even as a child, Sal had taken after
his father. Once, when I was only about seven, I was
walking home from school and our old neighbor
Mrs. Henning stopped me on the sidewalk.

"I know your daddy," she said. I knew she was talking about my stepfather, because my real father had died before I was born and had never lived in Bridgewater.

"Did you know that when Sal Signorelli was your age I saw him throw a whole litter of kittens into a bonfire?!" She shook her head, tears forming in her eyes. "And he did it with a smile on his face."

I ran home crying that day. When I asked my mother about this rumor, she told me it couldn't be true. Sal loved cats, and Mrs. Henning was a very old woman.

"No one really cared about him until I came along," my mom explained to me now. "If it weren't for us, who knows where he'd be?"

Probably in a county jail or mental institution, I thought.

"We help him *so* much," she said.

"Well, you would think he'd appreciate having a son," I said bitterly. "I mean, if he was lonely before, you know?"

"Oh, Luke, I'm sure he does. I'm sure he does." I noticed when she said this that she had a worried look on her face, as though she wasn't quite convinced herself.

Then, a few weeks later, everything changed for me.

om had a cleansing session scheduled for that afternoon out at the McKenzie farm, about an hour's drive away. In a cleansing, Mom believed she was getting rid of evil spirits that were haunting a place.

As she was leaving, she looked worried. I thought maybe she had fought with Sal again.

"What's wrong, Mom?" I asked.

"I don't know," she answered. She seemed distracted. "I'm feeling almost like I shouldn't go.

Just now, when I was getting my jacket, I thought I felt a hand on my shoulder holding me back."

"Come on, Mom," I said. "A hand? You're probably just worried that Sal will be mad at you again for going."

"Maybe you're right," she said. "Anyway, the McKenzies have been waiting for weeks for me. Mrs. McKenzie is at her wit's end . . . so many strange things happening in their house." She still looked pale, but she tried to smile at me. She kissed my forehead and went out the door.

Later that night, I sat outside, rocking on the old porch swing. A crisp breeze blew the leaves off the many trees that hid our old house from the road. Dark clouds drifted across the full moon. I was worried because it was almost midnight and Mom still hadn't come home from the farm. Sal, too, had not yet come back from picking up a body from a family's house over in Rockdale. He had been called around ten. Something seemed wrong.

I thought about calling Aisha, but I didn't want to worry her. Eventually, through the trees, I saw the hearse pull up and turn into the long, curved driveway that led to the funeral parlor on the side of the house. Sal got out and opened the back. He stopped when he noticed me sitting on the porch. He started walking toward me, looking at the ground. When he reached the porch, he looked right at me with a blank stare. I thought he was going to say something. But then he just turned around and started walking back to the hearse.

"Sal!" I followed after him. "What is it? What's going on?"

He glanced over his shoulder at me. "Listen," he mumbled, "There's been an accident. . . . Your mother's been killed."

My heart stopped for a moment. I felt cold, like my blood was draining out of me. Like someone was cutting into my stomach. I glanced at the open hearse. Had Sal brought her dead body home? I started toward it. Sal stopped me with his hand.

"That's not her," Sal quickly explained, "in the hearse, I mean. That's Mrs. Antonino. I went to pick up her body earlier, before the police reached me on my cell." He hung his head. I waited in disbelief and horror.

"Your mother's body . . ." he began. "I'm afraid there wasn't much left. . . . You see, there was a really bad fire. Your mother lost control of the car and crashed into a stone wall on a back road. No one saw the accident, but the car went up in flames. Everything was burned . . . but a few bone fragments." Sal had a strange, blank expression. "After I get Mrs. Antonino downstairs and prepped, I'll go collect the remains."

I stared at him, unable to speak. Hot tears burned lines down my face. I covered my cheeks with my hands. I couldn't believe I was crying in front of Sal. He was a monster. Did he even care that she was dead?

"I hate you! She hated you too! You *never* deserved her." I couldn't believe the words that

were coming out of my mouth. I'd never dared
to speak this way to Sal. But now I couldn't stop.
"You're a worthless excuse for a human being. You
made her life hell!"

I flinched a little, expecting Sal to come at me.
But he didn't even scream. He just stared. For a
second, I swear I saw a flicker of a smile pass over
his face.

"I'm sorry, boy," Sal said quietly. He shook his
head. "You'd best go to bed and get some rest. This
is a big shock for you."

And that was it.

He turned and shuffled back down the path
to the hearse. He hoisted Mrs. Antonio's black
body bag over his shoulder. Then he disappeared
through the side door that led down to the
mortuary prep room.

That night I couldn't sleep, thinking about
what my mother had said before she'd left that day.
Could it be that she was right about the Protectors
legend? Had her Protectors tried to warn her about

the accident? Was one of them responsible for the hand that had tried to stop her from going?

After a few hours, sleep finally took me. But I kept having nightmares. I saw my mother's car on fire. There was black smoke everywhere. I saw her body slumped over the steering wheel. I tried to scream, but no sound came out.

Then I was standing outside my house, and I saw a shadowy figure skulking around the side. Then it disappeared. I was so cold. The grass rustled behind me, and I turned to see Sal, standing tall with fury in his eyes. His arms were raised. He was holding an ax over his head, ready to strike.

I couldn't move—my feet were stuck to the spot. I heard my mother screaming from somewhere behind the house. "No, Sal, *noooooo!*"

I sat up in my bed, wide awake. My heart was pounding. I could swear I still heard the echo of my mother's scream in the distance.

I came downstairs in the morning to find that
my stepfather had been up all night. He'd been
preparing Mrs. Antonino's body and collecting
my mother's burnt remains. He said he had laid
her bones in a casket, now closed, in a corner of
the back room. I didn't want to look at them. My
mother's funeral service would take place the
following day.

I wondered how many people would come. We
had no family. My mother's parents died when she

was very young, and she didn't have any brothers or sisters. On my stepfather's side, I had only one uncle, Bert. Sal didn't speak to him anymore.

It seemed like everyone in Bridgewater and Rockdale showed up for my mother's funeral. Aisha and Lincoln were there early. Aisha didn't let go of my hand the whole day. It seemed like everyone had something nice to say about my mom.

"Your mother was a very special woman," Ms. Smith, a teacher at Bridgewater Elementary, told me. "She helped me through my mother's death."

"Let me know if you need anything," said Mr. Roswell, who worked at the auto shop.

"Your mother is looking out for you," explained Mrs. Winston. My mother had helped her connect with an aunt who had died several years ago.

It was nice to hear all these things. But I knew soon these people would all go home, and it would be just Sal and I. I thought again about the Protectors, and I wondered what my mom would say about her own case. There was no body left here, only bones. Would that count? Wouldn't she become my stepfather's Protector, not mine, since he had handled her remains before the burial? I dismissed these thoughts, though. Wasn't I still a rational thinker who didn't believe in spirits?

Near the end of the evening, Mrs. McKenzie hugged me. She cried like it was her own mother who'd died.

"It's so unfair!" she cried. "Her last act was to cleanse our house of evil, and then the evil followed her out!" Mrs. McKenzie struggled to keep control of her emotions. "You know, your mother knew something was wrong. She knew! Something strange, she said. . . . Her GPS was acting funny in the car. It kept showing her routes that would have taken her miles out of the way. She ignored it because she already knew the way. So strange, isn't it? She should have followed it anyway. If only she had followed it!"

I looked over at Sal, who was shaking hands and nodding as people offered their condolences.

His face looked empty. I saw Mrs. Morelli politely approach him. I cringed as I remembered the argument my parents had the day my mother went to visit with the old lady.

"Mr. Signorelli, I am so sorry for your loss," Mrs. Morelli said, and I could hear the sad sincerity in her soft voice. Sal just nodded, barely looking at her. She leaned in and whispered, "You know, she was so good at communicating with the dead, Mr. Signorelli. I am sure she is still here with you. Don't you worry."

He looked at Mrs. Morelli, and I instantly felt cold. In his eyes was the same flash of fury I had seen when he locked me in the casket room so many years ago. "Oh, I know that, Mrs. Morelli. I know she's still here."

As soon as the service was over, Sal and I carried the casket out into the backyard. We lowered it into a hole he had dug during the night. All of Sal's ancestors were buried in a little private cemetery in the far corner of the backyard.

I threw the first handful of dirt on top of the coffin. Tears were streaming down my face. I looked at Sal's face, but it was still vacant. It was like any other burial to him.

"Shouldn't we say something before—" I began.

"No!" he interrupted, now glaring at me. "Pick up that shovel and fill in the hole." He vanished into the house, where he went upstairs and locked himself in his room.

I did not see him again for three days.

Four days later, Sal brought in the first body since Mrs. Antonino. It was the former Frankie Davis, an obese man who'd died of diabetes. I went down to the prep room where Sal was getting things ready. Frankie was lying cold and stiff on a plastic sheet, his bluish-white skin almost glowing under the fluorescent light. His legs were swollen and purple. His head was turned sideways so that his wide-open eyes stared at me as I came in. His mouth gaped open, as though he were surprised. I shuddered when I saw him.

Death had never been personal for me before. Corpses had always been part of daily life. Now, with my mother dead, it was hard to think of Frankie as just another dead body. It gave me chills to see Frankie's lifeless eyes staring at me. I felt like running. Fortunately, Sal didn't really seem to want me around.

"What is it?" he growled at me when he saw me just standing there at the open door.

"I thought you might need help."

"It's a little late now. I've already got him down here. *That* was the hard part."

"How did you . . . ?"

"Never mind. I'm fine without you anyway." Sal began setting Frankie's facial features. He lifted Frankie's lip, which made it look like Frankie was sneering at me. I shuddered and left the room.

Weeks went by. I just assumed Sal was doing all the stuff my mother and I used to handle. He never asked for my help. I figured he was as glad to be away from me as I was to be away from him.

Eventually, I started noticing that all was *not* right with the family business. The bills were piling up unpaid on Sal's desk. There weren't many funeral services in the parlor either. I didn't see Sal going down to work in the prep room very much. Instead, he would sit for hours in the garage, drawing in a sketchbook. I'd never seen Sal draw before. That was his own weird way of grieving, I guessed.

One day when I got home from school, I found Sal in the garage, sketching. It had been weeks since our last funeral service. I needed to say something. This was our business. If we lost it, we would be broke.

"Hey," I said, trying to sound casual. I guess he hadn't seen me coming, because he jumped a little and closed his sketchbook. He looked up at me, his eyes vacant. He mumbled something I couldn't hear.

"No calls today?" I asked, but he did not reply. "Sal?"

He still didn't reply. His eyes were down now, and he wouldn't look up again. I went inside to check the messages myself. There were five in all, from families wanting to arrange funeral services. Two were from yesterday! I wrote down all the details and ran back out to the garage. Sal's notebook was open again.

"Um, these messages were on the voicemail. They sound important."

I held out the paper, but Sal did not reach for it. Without even looking up, he waved the paper away, grumbling.

"I think you should call them back. They'll go to another funeral home—"

"I'll take care of it!" he snapped. "I'm taking care of it."

I didn't want to push Sal too hard. I knew how that could backfire, so I didn't answer right away. I stood there in the doorway of the garage, weighing my options. Clearly, Sal was *not* taking care of it.

"Sal," I began hesitantly, "if you need help with the business—"

No response. He remained concentrated on his drawing. But I saw his forehead wrinkle a little. Maybe it was worry, irritation, or some other emotion I couldn't figure out.

"Maybe, at least I could take care of the paperwork, answer the phones and help make the arrangements—"

"Go away!" he roared. He stood up and lunged

at me. "Go away!" His lips were white around the edges. I ran out of the garage, my heart pounding, and I didn't look back.

Later that night, after Sal had gone to sleep, I found his sketchbook in the garage. I took a look at the drawings. In the sketchbook were drawings of people's faces, just from the neck up. I was surprised because they were pretty realistic drawings. I didn't know Sal had any artistic talent, but then again, there were probably a lot of things I didn't know about Sal.

But there was something strange about the drawings. The people looked limp. Their eyes stared straight ahead, looking glazed and sunken in. Many of their mouths hung open loosely. Then I realized—they were dead. Sal was drawing dead people. And many of them were bodies I'd seen before. There was Mrs. Chase before we'd wired her mouth shut. And young Kelly Hampton with her forehead smashed in from the car accident that killed her. I frantically flipped through the pages,

feeling sick and dizzy as I saw more and more
familiar faces. Why would Sal draw these people?

Then I stopped and stared at a page in the
middle of the sketchbook. It was my mother. But
she was thinner, and her hair was a mess around
her bony face. And unlike in the other drawings,
the eyes were bright and alert. My mother's mouth
was a tight, firm line. She was alive.

It had been almost a year since my mother's death.
I definitely wasn't over it. If anything, I was feeling
worse about it. The house felt strange, and it felt even
more off as the anniversary of her death approached.
Sal continued to draw in his sketchbook, but I hadn't
looked at it again. Once was enough.

That night I took a walk. I just felt like wandering.
I stepped outside, and the wind in the trees sounded
like whispers all around me. I could swear I heard
words. "Luke . . . go down . . . down!"

Was I hearing things? I pulled out my iPod—a gift from my mom—and pressed play. Then I walked to the end of my street and turned down Pleasantview Avenue.

It was my normal playlist—a mix of rock. But something weird happened in the middle of it. A track came on that I'd never heard before. It was a low voice singing, but a woman's voice. It sounded like a slow, sad folk song. The voice and the music sounded vaguely familiar, but I could barely hear it. It was muffled, and there was an echo and some static interference. Still, I could make out a dripping sound and something like chains rattling.

I hit the "back" button, but the playlist jumped back to the previous track. I scrambled to pull the iPod out of my pocket and try to get the weird song to play again, but it was gone.

I heard the chains again in my dreams that night. Or *was* it a dream? I was half awake and half asleep. I couldn't tell where the rattling was coming from. It reminded me of an episode of

Ghost Hunters I'd seen on TV recently, where they supposedly recorded a ghost rattling chains and moaning. It was so fake! Why would ghosts rattle chains anyway?

Dream or no dream, and ghost or no ghost, I definitely heard chains rattling. There was no moaning—or singing—but there were chains for sure. And it wasn't coming from outside.

Then I heard a creaking coming from inside the walls. I still didn't believe in ghosts. There had to be some rational explanation. But still, I stayed in my bed, wrapped in my blankets, not daring to move and not able to sleep.

What's wrong, man?" asked Lincoln as we walked out the doors of Bridgewater High toward the parking lot and Lincoln's car. Aisha was staying after school for drama club. "You look like you're totally dragging."

"Tired, I guess . . . didn't sleep too well." I paused. "Also . . . it's been almost a year since my mom died. I guess I've been thinking a lot about that."

"Hey, maybe she's still around," Lincoln offered.

"I'd like to believe it," I said, "but that was her thing, not mine."

"Come on," Lincoln insisted, "maybe she was right. Maybe she has become your Protector!" I had told Lincoln once about the Protectors, and he really stuck to the idea. He was so into it. He made me regret ever telling him.

"Look!" I snapped. "Even if that stuff is true, I was not the last one to touch her body. And, I don't even know if a few burnt-up bones count as a body." I stopped. I was starting to feel slightly sick.

"Hey, I'm sorry, man. I was just trying to cheer you up. Listen, maybe you need to get out a little. I was thinking of having a few people over tonight to hang out, if you wanna come."

"I don't think so, Lincoln. Thanks anyway."

"Why not?"

"I just don't really feel like it," I said. Was it really that hard to figure out why?

"It will be fun," Lincoln said as we got in his car.

"You can bring Aisha. And I want you to meet this girl I'm seeing."

I raised my eyebrows. Lincoln had a new girlfriend every month. He laughed at my expression.

"No, she's really great. Her name is Sheila. Come on, man. It'll be fun! You never go anywhere. That's, like, scientifically proven to be bad for your health. I won't take no for an answer."

I sighed. "Okay, I'll be there." Maybe I could leave early.

Lincoln was right. I never went out. But I must have been feeling more alone than ever in our big, old, empty house with only Sal for company. I guess, on some level, I wanted to be around people—normal people.

I walked over to Aisha's house to pick her up, and then we walked together to Lincoln's. Aisha was all dressed up. She was so happy to be going to a party with me that it made me feel a little guilty. I hadn't taken her anyplace nice in a long time.

I couldn't believe my eyes when we got there. It turned out "a few people" meant half the student body of Bridgewater High and the two neighboring schools. All around, kids were dancing, talking, screaming, laughing. Aisha and I found Lincoln in a corner, talking to a girl with long blond hair.

Aisha poked me in the ribs as we walked over. "Is this girlfriend five or six of this year?" she whispered. I smiled and shrugged.

"My man!" Lincoln shouted when he saw me. "This is Sheila." Lincoln put an arm around the girl he'd been talking to. She was smiling and holding a cup of some colorful punch. "Sheila, this is Luke and Aisha."

"Hey," said Sheila, smiling and rocking a little where she stood. Her face was flushed pink. It was pretty obvious that she had been drinking—a lot.

At the sound of my name, a skinny kid with bad acne and a baseball hat whipped around. "Luke Signorelli?" he asked.

"Yeah . . ." I said.

"You're the kid who pickles bodies in his basement, right?"

"Fitch!" said Lincoln, annoyed.

Fitch continued. "Dude, I want to hear *all* about it."

I looked at Lincoln, who shrugged. "Luke, this is Jim Fitchburg. He goes to Rockdale High with Sheila." I smiled weakly at him. I didn't expect anyone to be so interested in embalming.

"So, how do you do it? I mean, do you cut up the bodies and stuff?" Fitch asked.

"Well, sort of. It's kind of hard to explain."

"Sheila," Lincoln said, laughing, "you be the cadaver, and Luke can show us how it's done."

Sheila cleared off a coffee table and lay down on top of it. I acted out the whole process. A small crowd started gathering around me. Every cut with my imaginary scalpel met with hoots of cheers and laughter. At first I felt good. It was fun getting attention for my weird set of skills, even if they were only cheering because they'd all been drinking so much. But all of a sudden I was freaked out. It was too real or something—Sheila playing dead on the coffee table.

"Okay, okay, that's it," I announced.

"Come on, finish!" Aisha said.

I looked up, and I saw a sea of laughing faces.

"No, no really, that's it—all we do next is fix up the hair . . ." My hands were clammy as I tried to reach for Sheila's hair. I felt like throwing up. "That's it." I jumped up and ran outside. I sat down in a chair by the pool, trying to catch my breath.

A few minutes later, Aisha was there. She touched me lightly on the shoulder.

"Luke, are you okay?" she asked. She was trying not to be dramatic, but I knew how worried she was. That was the thing about Aisha—she couldn't hide anything she felt.

"I don't think so," I said, looking away. I wanted to explain, but how could I? Whatever was happening to me I couldn't even explain to myself, much less another person, no matter how close she was.

I hadn't had any nightmares about my mother's death in a long time. But that night, they started again.

In my dream, everything was black and silent. Suddenly, I could see my mother trapped inside a casket, banging from the inside. She was screaming to get out as Sal and I lowered her into the ground in the backyard and began throwing dirt on her casket.

I woke up in a sweat. I swear, I could still hear her voice. I heard her muffled screams and banging through the night.

The next morning, Sheila's body was at my house.

The hospital morgue brought Sheila over. Sal was locked in his room, so there was no one to see to her but me.

I couldn't believe it. Apparently, after Aisha and I left the party, Sheila kept drinking. She and Fitch went walking out on Bluff Island. They were walking near Dead Man's Cave when Sheila lost her balance and fell. She died instantly on the rocks below.

Lincoln texted me. *Did u hear??*

I texted him back, my fingers trembling. *She's here.*

In ten minutes, Lincoln was ringing the bell and banging on the door. "Let me see her! Let me see her!" he begged. He looked like hell, with dark circles under his eyes and the same clothes from yesterday. "It's my fault! I shouldn't have let her drink so much. . . ."

"Lincoln, just go home and get some rest or something." I didn't know what to say. I didn't get that gene from my mother, the one that lets you know how to help people when they're at their worst. "I don't think it's a good idea for you to see her."

"Please!" he begged. "I need to, Luke. Can't you do this for me?"

To be honest, the thought of working on Sheila alone in the basement had me sick inside. Especially when I thought about our performance the night before. I wanted to say yes to Lincoln, but I was afraid the sight of stiff, dead, bruised-up Sheila would be too much for him. It was almost too much for *me*.

"Lincoln, she's really not looking . . . herself. Maybe you should wait till I finish with her."

"I can help you. Please! I don't care. I can handle it. I've seen pretty awful stuff before, Luke, believe me."

I did believe him. Lincoln's family was a little shady.

I led Lincoln downstairs to the prep room. The fluorescent light glinted off the white tiles on the walls and illuminated Sheila's broken, bloody body on the embalming table. Lincoln took one look, reeled backward, and fainted cold on the floor. I waited for him to wake up. Then I carefully helped him up into a chair on one side of the room. You could tell he was going to have a bruise on the left side of his head.

"Do you want ice?" I said, though what I was thinking was *I told you.*

Lincoln just looked back at me with bleary, half-closed eyes. "I'm okay," he murmured.

I uncovered Sheila's body and began spraying it with disinfectant and washing off the crusted blood. Then I picked up some tools for setting her facial features. Just then, the lights started to flicker, and I felt the room shake.

"What's that?" cried Lincoln, snapping out of his daze and jumping out of the chair.

"I don't know," I replied as the room stopped shaking and the lights steadied. Everything was suddenly very quiet. I looked back at Sheila and saw that her abdomen was strangely puffed out. Her eyes popped open. Lincoln gasped and cried out a little. It looked like she was looking at us.

Her mouth was beginning to open. Slowly, a low moan issued from her throat.

"He . . . eee . . . lll herrr . . ." she moaned.

"Wha-what did she say?" asked Lincoln in a tiny, terrified voice.

"Nothing, man," I tried to reassure him—and myself. "It happens sometimes, when a body has been sitting for some time. The mouth can open, and sometimes there is gas trapped inside the body that needs to come out. . . ."

But I didn't even believe my own words. No, this was something else. I could tell by the way she was looking right at us and how the moan sounded so much like words.

Lincoln was shaking. "Dude, I gotta get outta here!"

"Wait, Lincoln—" It was too late. Lincoln was up the stairs and out the front door before I could finish my sentence.

Now it was just me and Sheila. At least she looked dead again. She just stared ahead blankly, her mouth still hanging open. What did she say? "Hell herrr . . . ?" What did that mean, that Sheila was in hell? That hell was *here*? Or did she mean "help her"? Help *who*?

"Help who?!" I shouted at Sheila. I felt a breeze pass through the windowless room.

It was another rough night. More nightmares. This time, dead Sheila sat up on the embalming table and asked me to tell her all about my line of work. I looked around, and a crowd of kids from Bridgewater and Rockdale High was standing in the prep room, waiting. But they weren't laughing. They were just staring at me silently.

"Come on, Luke! Show them what you do," Sheila said, her head cocked to one side because of her broken neck, bruises all over her face and arms.

Then my mother came in. She was so thin, and her clothes were ragged and filthy. Her pale skin contrasted with the dark circles under her eyes, and her hair was ratty. She was holding a burnt thighbone in her hand.

"Luke," she said, "what about me?" Sheila and all the other kids turned to look at her. "What about my body, Luke?"

I woke up gasping for air. It was three in the morning.

I went down to the kitchen for a glass of milk. I sat at the kitchen table, trying just to not think for a minute, when I felt the light shifting around me. I turned. A shadowy figure was coming up the stairs. I looked up and saw a pair of yellowed eyes, wide open.

"Sal!" I cried.

He was carrying a plate of food and a bottle of milk. Since my mother's death, "food" basically consisted of sliced bread, cold meats, and fruit—nothing that required much preparation or cooking.

Sal jumped the way he did when I saw him sketching in the garage. A few grapes rolled off the plate as it shook for a second in his hand. He didn't bother to pick them up. He started forward, as if to pass me, without a word.

"Sal?" I said.

"What?! What do you want?!" he barked, whipping his head around to face me.

I walked up to him. "I . . . I just . . ." I began.

"Get out of my way. Just get out of my way!" He pushed me so hard I fell to the side. I landed on the stairs, crumpled against the railing. He stomped up the stairs and into his room.

Sheila's wake was awful.

Many of the kids who had been at the party came, as well as Sheila's entire family and all of their friends. Not one of them acknowledged me. Not even Fitch, who had been so chummy with me at the party. *Especially* not Fitch. He avoided looking at me the entire time. Even Lincoln did not seem to want anything to do with me.

"Hey, man," I said to him, as he came through the front door of the funeral parlor. "You okay?" I awkwardly patted him on the shoulder.

"Hey," he said. Did he actually turn away from me? I pretended not to notice.

"I think she looks pretty good," I said, nodding toward Sheila's casket at the back of the room. I guess this wasn't the right thing to say. I saw Lincoln's eyes dart toward the coffin. Then he closed them, as if he were remembering something very painful. He turned around, pivoting on one heel. He walked right out of the funeral parlor and didn't come back.

I couldn't blame him for being freaked out. I was pretty freaked out myself—and she wasn't even my girlfriend. But still, I felt close to her. We were connected in some way I didn't understand. I briefly wondered if she was my Protector, but I quickly dismissed the thought.

Aisha couldn't make it to the wake, but she came over later that afternoon. We met outside my house so Sal wouldn't see us. He was still mad at me for sneaking off to Lincoln's party without telling him. It was strange. He wanted me to stay out of his way, but he never wanted me to go away either.

Aisha and I slipped into the hearse in the driveway, where it was warmer.

"Are you doing okay?" Aisha asked. "I've been worried about you."

I shrugged. She leaned over and gave me a hug. That almost made me cry. Why is it that the tears always come *after* the worst part of something? I'd felt like a leper at Sheila's wake, and I'd been worried Aisha would treat me the same way. But she didn't. Of course she didn't.

"Are you sure we can't go inside?" she asked after a minute. "Your stepfather has always liked me. I don't think he'd mind."

I shook my head. "I think he's gotten worse," I said. "He used to just argue with my mom and me. But now he doesn't even go see his friends.

He doesn't talk to anyone. He doesn't work. He's just mad . . . all the time."

"Maybe he's grieving," she said.

"Maybe . . . or maybe, he's really going crazy."

Just then, the garage opened in front of us. My stepfather stood glaring. Aisha seemed to straighten up in her seat a bit. I realized this was the first time she had seen him since my mother's funeral. I thought about how he must look to her. He had dark circles under his eyes, and his mouth was pulled into a hard frown. In his left hand he clutched his closed sketchbook.

"What is this?" he asked gruffly. "What are you doing in here?"

"Oh, uh, I was just . . ." I muttered.

Sal glared at Aisha. "I don't want anyone around here! Get her out!" he roared.

I didn't say anything. I just got out of the car. Aisha quickly followed my lead.

Sal stood there for a moment. Then he sat down in his chair and opened his sketch pad.

"I'm gonna go," Aisha said quietly.

"Sorry," I whispered. "Bye."

She ran home, looking back only once. I saw the familiar worry in her eyes.

As I turned back toward Sal, I heard the phone ring inside. He didn't make a move to get it, so I walked past him into the house and picked it up in the office. It was a business call.

"Sal," I said, walking into the garage, "that was Mr. Abernethy at 17 Willow Street. He needs us to come pick up his mother, who just expired."

"Well, I'm busy right now."

"I told him we would come. . . ."

Sal didn't even look up. I pictured him sketching my own dead body and shuddered.

"I think I'll go get her, then," I said after a moment. It was pretty obvious by now that I was the only one capable of doing any work around the house. I threw up my arms and headed for the hearse.

"So, you like that girl of yours?" Sal asked suddenly.

I just stared at him.

"*Be careful.* A man's got to look out for himself."

I wasn't even sure he was talking to me.

Mr. Abernethy looked a little shocked to see me walk up the steps, but I assured him that I was now officially helping my stepfather at the funeral home. I explained that my stepfather wasn't well lately, which was no exaggeration, really. I added that we weren't bringing in enough money to hire any additional help—also true.

Mr. Abernethy helped me use the gurney to carry his mother out and put her in the back of the hearse. He said he'd come by the following morning to discuss the funeral arrangements. Sheila's funeral was that day as well. I knew Sal wasn't going to handle things, so I was going to have to miss school.

That night, I set about fixing up Alice Abernethy for her viewing. Her eyelids were only half-closed, and I could see the whites of her eyes.

As I started to turn on the embalming machine, I heard a rustling on the table. I turned. Alice was twitching.

A year ago, the sight of a body twitching would not have fazed me—it happens sometimes, naturally. But this was different. The old lady's body gave one final jerk, and her right arm flopped upward and bent back. Her fingers had all curled toward her palm except for her index finger. It looked like she was pointing behind her head toward the supply closet.

First Sheila, and now this. I couldn't help but think that someone was trying to send me a message. *My Protectors?* I thought. *My mother?* No. I couldn't go there. "Crazy," I said out loud, just as another cold breeze passed through the room.

I walked over to the supply closet, just in case. Slowly, I opened the door. It was too dark to see. I pulled the chain that hung from a light fixture on the closet ceiling. I saw the usual: shelves on three sides filled with bottles of embalming fluid, disinfectant spray, creams, chemicals, and cleaning supplies. There was a black rubber mat on the floor, a broom, a mop, and a bucket. Relieved, I closed the door and turned back toward Alice.

My eyes widened at what I saw as I began working on her skin. It seemed to be having a reaction to the cream I had applied. Her flesh looked splotchy, with red patches like some kind of rash. *That's weird,* I thought. *She's dead. Why is her skin having a reaction?* I pulled the sheet back, but what I saw made me lose my grip. Across her abdomen, in red welts, was written my mother's name. *Penny.*

I went outside and walked around the block, breathing deeply. What did all of this mean? The nightmares, the screams in the night that had sounded so real, the creaking in the wall, the rattling chains, the voices in the wind, the track on my iPod, Sheila's breathy words, Alice's rash and pointing finger. . . . Was I going crazy? Was I going to end up like Sal, sketching images of dead people in my garage and angry at the whole world?

No. Lincoln had been there. He had heard that voice say "help her" through Sheila's mouth. Isn't that why he'd left at a run? I pulled out my cell phone and started to text. But then I stopped and put the phone back in my pocket. What was I thinking? Lincoln wouldn't want to talk about that. Not now, while he was still in shock about Sheila's death. Probably not *ever*!

I thought of talking about this to Aisha, but I couldn't bring myself to do it. She'd probably think I was going crazy. She had already looked so shocked by Sal's behavior. I couldn't put this on her.

As I came back to the house, I saw Sal's hunched silhouette near the far wall of his room, but I couldn't quite see what he was doing. It looked like he was climbing up onto something—or maybe into something—just beyond the edge of the window frame.

I reluctantly returned to Alice. She was exactly as I'd left her, but her rash was gone. *Maybe it was never even there,* I thought. *Maybe I was hallucinating.*

I worked as fast as I could to drain the blood and pump in the chemicals. I watched nervously for another sign, but nothing happened.

It was one in the morning by the time I had finished and got to bed. Sleep came over me immediately, but I was soon awakened by creaking in the walls.

It's just old house noises, I tried to convince myself. The noise stopped, and I fell back into an uneasy sleep with uneasy dreams.

I was on the front lawn. And there they were, coming toward me. A crowd of dead bodies, some of the people who'd died years ago, embalmed and dressed for their funerals.

There was little Darlene Winkler, dead at age six. She was wearing a frilly white dress and carrying a porcelain doll that looked just like her. There was Mr. Morelli in his blue suit, carrying a clear plastic bag that held his organs. Old Dr. Miller was coming too. He wore his tuxedo and held his medical bag. Mrs. Chase traipsed in her flowered housedress, barefoot. There were others, but I didn't recognize them. Their eyes were all sealed, and their mouths were closed with wires and sutures. They stumbled toward me blindly, moaning through their closed lips, desperate to tell me something but unable to.

I tried to run, but something was holding me

down. "What do you want?" I shouted at them, but my voice came out as a whisper.

A loud song brought me out of my nightmare. It was coming from my alarm clock radio. *Why is it going off at 3 A.M.?* I thought as I fumbled for the power button. *I didn't even set the alarm!* It was tuned to some R&B station that I definitely hadn't selected. A woman sang, "He's got me where he wants me, ohh, but I ain't gonna stay. Now that you have found me, baby, won't you come my way?"

I hit every damn button, but the radio wouldn't shut off. "I'm tired of being a prisoner, baby, break me from these chains. . . ." Finally I grabbed the radio, tearing the plug from the socket. I threw it across the room, and it shattered against the wall.

I couldn't stop shaking.

I stopped going to school. All of my time was spent answering the phone, making arrangements, driving the hearse for pickups and funeral processions, preparing bodies, and running wakes. I almost never saw Aisha. I was kind of surprised she hadn't dumped me yet. I guess she knew I was going through some stuff.

I was the one holding everything together, and I felt like I was coming apart.

The day before the first anniversary of my mother's death, I found a card in the mail, addressed to Salvatore Signorelli V and Luca Signorelli. *Luca.* No one *ever* called me that—my real first name. I flipped over the envelope. "Alberto Signorelli." The address was in Connecticut. *Uncle Bert?* As far as I knew, I'd never even met my step-uncle. I barely even knew anything about him.

I ripped open the envelope and pulled out the card. It was a sympathy card.

Dear brother Sal and nephew Luca,

I am so very sorry that this card arrives so late, but I only just heard about your family tragedy from an old Bridgewater acquaintance I ran into this morning. Why did you not call me or write to me, brother? I know we have had our troubles, but family is family.

Luca, we do not know one another, and I deeply regret that. However, I can assure you that it was not

my choice. I hope that we can someday remedy this
sad situation.

I am very sorry for the loss that you both have
suffered, and I hope that your wounds have healed
somewhat now that a year has passed. Time cannot
heal all wounds, but I hope that it might heal some.

I am here if you need me.

Sincerely,
Bért

I took the card inside and left it on the kitchen
counter for Sal to see. Stuffing the addressed
envelope in my pocket, I decide to Google my
step-uncle. I thought maybe he went and opened
another funeral service business somewhere
else, but no. He was actually an obstetrician. He
delivered babies. He ushered people into this life
rather than ushering them out.

He was also married and had three kids. I
actually had family somewhere. But my stomach
turned a little when I thought about meeting them.

What if Uncle Bert turned out to be just like Sal?

On the back of the envelope, I jotted down the phone number I found for Bert's medical practice in Connecticut.

I didn't think things could get worse. It was the anniversary of my mother's death, and I was certain that someone was watching me. Following me. I could almost feel them breathing down my neck.

It was a Saturday, 6:00 A.M. I woke to my bed rocking; it felt like the whole house was shaking. I held onto the edge of my mattress, confused and sweating. The motion stopped after a minute, and I got out of bed as if I'd been pushed.

As I walked down the stairs, I passed the framed photographs of my mother in her wedding gown and Sal in his tuxedo. Suddenly, Sal's photo fell to the floor. The glass in the frame shattered. *Dammit,* I thought. *I'm probably gonna get blamed for this!* As I picked up the glass, a piece sliced across my hand. My blood spilled onto the photograph. I tried wiping it off, but it seeped into the matte paper, leaving the image of my stepfather covered in blood.

I bandaged my hand, then swept up the mess. Not knowing what else to do, I went to put the ruined photograph in the trash. When I lifted the lid, I saw my uncle's card in the heap.

The cold breeze passed by again. I could see the hairs rising on my arms.

I pressed my uninjured hand over my forehead. *This is insane,* I kept thinking. *Am I actually going crazy? I have to get outta here.* I headed for the front door. I put on my headphones. But then I took them off and pulled out my cell phone. I needed to talk to someone. I dialed Lincoln. He didn't pick up. I dialed again. It rang and rang. I dialed again, but this time the call went straight to voicemail. *He doesn't want to talk to me,* I thought. I sent him a text, though I didn't think he would answer me. *Call me. I need to talk 2 u.*

Suddenly my phone started ringing. It was Aisha. "Want to go for a walk?" she asked.

Aisha was at my house in fifteen minutes. She crossed her arms tightly across her chest as she stood in the doorway. I knew she was worried that my stepfather would emerge from somewhere. I quickly grabbed my coat, and we rushed out the door.

It was a misty morning. It seemed like the whole neighborhood was still sleeping. Aisha pulled her coat tightly around her body and shivered a little. We hadn't seen each other in a week. I'd missed her.

"I'm really worried about you," Aisha said after a while of walking in silence.

I'm really worried about me too, I thought. But instead I said, "Yeah, don't be worried. I'll be fine."

Aisha shook her head. "You shouldn't be living with that guy. Your stepdad is a jerk."

"I agree. But where else am I going to go?"

"Luke, he could be dangerous or something. He has so much rage."

Suddenly I thought of Uncle Bert's letter. "My Uncle Bert sent me a letter. He's my stepdad's brother. But I haven't met him."

Aisha stopped on the sidewalk and looked right at me. "I really think you should call him."

I nodded. One more thing to think about.

We talked for almost an hour before I reluctantly said good-bye to Aisha and headed home. My stepfather would be waking up soon. He would be angry if I wasn't there.

When I went through the front door into my house, I was greeted by a sharp smack across the face. It sent me staggering to the side.

"What is the meaning of this?" shouted Sal. He was holding his bloodstained photo in the hand that hadn't smacked me.

"I didn't do it. It just fell." I winced as I felt my face, making sure nothing was too badly damaged.

"It just fell? It just fell?! Sure it did! It's been hanging there for fifteen years, and today it just fell."

"Well, yes. . . ." I backed away.

He pushed me toward his office. "I've had enough of this. You've always been against me. Always!"

I looked at him, not knowing what to say. I was against *him*?

We reached his office, and he grabbed me gruffly by the arm. He opened the closet. I held my breath, remembering the night he locked me in the casket room. I struggled, but he was stronger. He was going to lock me in there, and this time there was no one to come home and help me.

But he let go of my arm and pointed up to a shelf at the top of the closet.

"You go through those boxes," he said, "and you find that negative. You are going to replace that photo, exactly as it was, or you will be very, very sorry." Then he went outside, slamming the door behind him. I heard him drive away in the hearse.

I set to going through the boxes. It was weird. I found photo after photo of the wedding, but there were only photos of my mother and Sal. There weren't any wedding guests. It took almost an hour for me to find the negative I was looking for. I had to hold each strip up to the light and examine each little square image.

I did find a few old pictures showing Sal as a little kid, including one of him with his parents and baby Bert. My mother had shown me this photo before. I'd never noticed before that no one was smiling. Sal is looking directly at the camera, as though he is angry with it. He looks a lot like his father, who is also scowling. His mother is looking off into the distance somewhere. Bert is crying.

I stared at Bert for a long time, wondering whether to follow Aisha's advice and call him. What did I have to lose?

I put everything away. Then I ran upstairs and pulled out the envelope I had saved in my pocket the day before. Without hesitation, I dialed Uncle Bert's number. After several rings, I heard a man's voice on the other end.

"This is Dr. Signorelli," he said. The voice of a busy man without a lot of time to spare for a phone call.

It took me several seconds to be able to say, "Alberto . . . ?"

"Yes, who is this?"

"This is . . . your nephew. Luke. Luca."

There was a pause. "Luke!" said Bert, his voice friendlier now. "So . . . you got my card."

"Yes, I read it. Thank you."

"It's good to hear from you, Luke. How is everything? How is my brother?"

"Sal? He's . . . not doing so well, actually."

"Oh," said Bert. He sounded concerned but not surprised. "I'm sorry to hear that. . . . Are you okay?"

I hesitated. This was my first conversation with Bert. I didn't know how much I should tell him. But I was feeling desperate. "I don't know, actually. Things are a little strange right now."

"Strange, how? What's going on?"

I was silent for a second. "Umm . . ."

"You know what, Luke? How about I stop by Bridgewater for lunch tomorrow afternoon? Say around noon? Is there a place I can meet you?"

"Um, sure," I said. "Let's meet at Chowder Hut, by the marina."

"I'll see you there," Burt said cheerfully. "Oh, and don't bring Sal."

"Okay," I said, although I didn't know how I was going to explain my absence to my stepfather.

13

As it turned out, Sal had plans to be out on Sunday until late afternoon. I didn't know where he was going, but I didn't really want to know. For a change, I felt lucky. I could easily meet Bert without worrying about Sal the whole time.

At noon I arrived at the diner. I hadn't seen a recent photograph of Bert, but I knew him immediately. He looked a lot like Sal, only he had more hair and he was smiling. Bert picked me out too.

"I can't believe you are sixteen!" he exclaimed, pulling me into a bear hug. "You're growing up fast."

We took a seat at a table near the window. "So," Bert said after we had ordered some food. "How bad is it?"

I was surprised that he jumped right to the point. I guess he knew Sal better than I did. I told him all about how Sal was acting.

"I'm sorry, Luke," Bert began, "but I must say, I am not all that surprised."

"No?" I asked.

"No. Let me tell you something, Luke. Your stepfather and I never got along, even as kids. Things were tough. Our parents were not very giving people, emotionally. I realize now that they both were probably mentally ill, but when you're a kid you don't understand those things. You think if your parents are behaving strangely, it must be because of something you did."

I nodded. I used to think that way about Sal.

I thought it was my fault he got angry. Luckily, I know better now.

"Anyway," Bert continued. "Sal was always trying really hard to get the approval of Mama and Papa. He was three years older than me. I think when I came along, he saw me as competition for their attention. So he was always trying to put me down in front of them.

"Then, when I was around seven and Sal was ten, Mama left us. Just like that, without a word. We never saw or heard from her again. I was pretty upset, as you might imagine, but Sal, he took it *really* badly. After that, he was even meaner to me than he had been before, as though it were my fault that she had left. He even said to me once, 'You drove her away!' Our father took it badly too. He become more short-tempered. He didn't spend much time with us except to teach us the family business."

"What about my mother?" I asked. "When did Sal meet her?"

"When Sal was nineteen, your mother got a job with us, doing the hair and makeup for the deceased. You were just a baby then. Penny was a very interesting girl—very spiritual. Sal fell for her hard, and he was very possessive of her. Couldn't stand it if I talked to her or even looked at her. One time he locked me in the supply closet for three hours just because he had caught me alone with her in the embalming room."

I flashed to my own night in the casket room.

"Now Penny, she was a kindhearted girl, and I think she saw Sal as a troubled soul who needed her help. More so after our father took his own life the following year. With both our parents gone, and Sal in charge, I started feeling pushed out. Eventually, I couldn't take it anymore. I left when I was only eighteen. When I had a new address, I sent it to my brother, but he never wrote me. He didn't even invite me to his wedding. I don't know who he *did* invite."

"Not too many people," I replied, thinking of the wedding photos I'd seen yesterday. "Bert?" I began.

"Yes?"

"Can I ask you something?"

"Go ahead."

"Do you think Sal is . . . *dangerous*?"

Bert looked down at his coffee cup. "I don't know, Luke. There were times when I did worry. And when I left, I worried about you and your mother. Over the years, I tried to make contact with her, and even with you. But Sal always stood in the way."

The words hung in the air between us. My head was reeling. Sal's own brother thought he might be capable of hurting someone. My mind went back to the night of my mother's death. It was all so strange the way it happened. He had been angry with her that day, hadn't he? And he was so cold and unfeeling at her funeral. And then there was my nightmare with my mother screaming and him with the ax.

"Bert, do you think Sal could have hurt my mother?" I blurted out. "I mean, the accident she died in, could it have not been an accident?"

Bert sighed and glanced around the diner. "He loved her so very much. I don't think he could have . . . *killed* her," he said.

But I wasn't so sure. He had become so violent. They had always been arguing.

The waitress came over with our food. When she set my pancakes in front of me, I nearly gasped. Someone had poured maple syrup over them already. The amber lines of syrup clearly spelled *closet.*

"Bert . . ." I mumbled. I looked up at him, but he didn't seem to notice anything unusual. "I've got to go."

As I ran home, I kept thinking, *I never saw her body.* I remembered Mrs. Antonino, who had also died that night. *I never saw* her *body, either.*

And now, *closet* had been written on my pancakes. Either I really was going crazy, or someone was trying to tell me something. I didn't care anymore. I had to follow the clues, whatever they meant.

I ran all the way home and to the supply closet in the prep room. I found what I had missed before.

The wall at the back of the closet had obviously been boarded over. I banged on the wood and heard a hollow echo behind it. I remembered seeing a similar panel in the kitchen a long time ago. An old opening had been boarded over, and the pantry had been put in front of it.

Now that I thought about it, the kitchen was directly over the prep room. I ran upstairs and searched behind the pantry. There it was—the same kind of board in the wall. The two must be connected somehow. I wondered if there was another on the third floor. That would be in my stepfather's room. Just the thought of going in there made beads of sweat prickle on my forehead. But I knew I had to act, and now was my only chance.

I ran up the stairs and turned down the hallway. I hadn't gone into that room in years, even when my mother was still alive. That was Sal's territory, and I instinctively knew it was not my place to enter. Even now, I could barely force myself to open the door. I imagined him sitting in there, waiting.

Maybe he hadn't gone out after all. Maybe it was all just a trap. I turned the knob and pushed the door slowly open, half expecting him to jump out at me.

But the room was empty. I turned to the wall directly above the pantry. A large mirror hung in the center. I went over and pushed it aside. And there it was—an opening. Only this one wasn't boarded up. It had a wooden door on it, with iron hinges. I carefully took the mirror down, my curiosity burning.

Inside the door hung a wooden platform suspended on ropes, with two extra ropes hanging down on one side. I tugged on one of these. It was attached to some kind of pulley system that made the platform go up and down. I realized it was a dumbwaiter. I'd seen those in old movies. People used to use them for transporting things around the house. This one looked ancient. It must have been part of the original house.

I grabbed the rope again and tugged on it. An all-too familiar creaking sound echoed inside the wall. I remembered seeing Sal's silhouette hunched over something when I'd looked up at his lit window. He must have been climbing onto the small platform. He was using the dumbwaiter to transport himself! But *where*? The other openings in the kitchen and the prep room were both boarded up.

There must be another level, I thought. *Go down.* In my mind, I heard the voice on the wind. *Go down.*

I climbed inside the little elevator and began pulling at the rope. It eased me down, down, down the dark shaft. I wished I had thought to bring a flashlight. It was pitch black. The walls felt like they were closing in on me. I started to panic, then— *thunk*—I had reached the bottom.

I shoved the door, and it swung open. Before me was a pitch-black expanse that smelled of mildew and ancient dust. I couldn't see a thing. All I could hear was the sound of water dripping and echoing throughout the silent space.

A hand pushed me forward. I spun around and thrashed my arms, but no one was there. I thought of the hand that had grabbed my mother the day she'd died. Were the Protectors here? And if so, what danger did I face?

Whispers and murmurs swirled around my head. Voices were speaking, but I couldn't make out words. I walked forward slowly. I noticed a faint sliver of light along the floor in the far corner to my left.

I stumbled toward it. Then I heard another familiar sound—chains rattling. I groped my way toward the light until my hands were touching what felt like an unfinished plywood wall.

I heard a low moan, and I jumped. There was someone behind it!

"Wh-who's in there?" I whispered.

I heard a woman's voice, but it was so weak that I couldn't hear any words.

I felt all along the wooden wall. I came to a corner, turned, and felt along the other side. This was some kind of wooden enclosure. And there was a door. I found a handle and tried to turn it. It was locked. I kicked at the door, pushed it with my shoulder, but it would not budge. The voice whimpered on the other side.

Who was there? With all my strength, I threw my entire body against the door again and again. Finally, the plywood cracked at the lock, and I pushed the door in.

I froze at the sight in front of me. A thin and sickly woman was crumpled on the floor in chains. Her long hair was tangled, and her clothes were dirty rags. A small lamp in one corner of the enclosure threw enough light on her that I could see her face when she looked up at me.

"*Mom?*"

Her face was so thin and pale, I could barely recognize her. But it was definitely her. She smiled weakly at me.

"Luke!" she said in almost a whisper. "I knew you would come! They told me you would come!"

"*Who* told you, Mom?" I ran to her and threw my arms around her. I could feel her whole body shaking as she hugged me back with her frail, thin arms. I was sobbing too. My mother was *alive*! But just barely.

"My Protectors," she said. "They've been speaking to you, Luke. But not many people are willing to listen to them. Most people never get their messages."

"*Your* Protectors!" I said. Of course! Now that I knew she was alive, it made perfect sense.

A creaking echoed across the basement, and we looked at each other in fear. Sal was pulling up the dumbwaiter.

"Luke!" my mother cried. "Listen to me. You've got to get out of here before he comes down. You've got to hide!"

"Where? It's so dark I can't see anything! Isn't there another way out of this basement?

"Not anymore, I don't think," she whispered.

"Mom, I need to get you out of here!" I said. Then I noticed a shackle around her left ankle. She was chained to the wall.

Frantic, I left the enclosure and started feeling around the basement's damp cement walls for another door or a staircase—anywhere to hide. There couldn't be a door directly to the outside, since we were far underground. Even the level above, where we did the embalming, was below ground. Still, there had to be a staircase, somewhere.

The creaking in the wall stopped. The dumbwaiter had reached my stepfather's room. I kept feeling around the walls, walking through old cobwebs. Once or twice I brushed against some multi-legged creature that scurried away at the touch of my fingers.

Creeeeak . . .

Then I reached it—a staircase, not much more than a stepladder. I tried going up, but it just went straight to a trapdoor in the ceiling. I pushed and pulled and slammed it with my shoulder, but nothing happened.

The creaking stopped again with a *thunk!* I heard the door swing open and bang against the basement wall. Next came the sound of feet landing on the ground. Then footsteps. I could see a flashlight leading my stepfather toward my mother. My heart was pounding, but I felt paralyzed.

Where is he?" I heard my stepfather shout. "I know he's down here!"

"Please, Sal . . ."

"You always take his side, don't you? You and that boy—you always wanted to push me out!"

Chains were rattling and dragging across the floor. My mother screamed, "No! Sal, please, it's not true. We never—"

"Shut up!" he shouted. "Where is he?"

I heard a muffled thud as he threw my mother

onto the floor. Something inside me snapped. Now that I knew she was alive, I couldn't let him hurt her anymore.

I raced toward the enclosure. It was dark, but the faint light from my mother's lamp shining through the now-opened door was enough for me to see what was in front of me—my enraged stepfather. He was holding something long and metal in his right hand.

My reflexes kicked in. I tried to whip past Sal to get to my mother, but he grabbed me by the shirt collar with his left hand. He raised his right hand. I could see the metal object better now. It was the trocar—the sharp, pointed instrument we used to drain bodies.

I kicked one of Sal's knees as hard as I could. He buckled to the ground, losing his hold on my collar. I rolled away. As he righted himself, I groped in the darkness for something—anything—I could use to hurt him.

He was coming toward me, the glinting trocar still in hand. He shouted, "I've had enough of this, enough of you!" I could feel his saliva spraying my face. "She always loved you more than she loved me! Always!"

"She could have loved both of us!" I screamed back at him. "Don't you see? You pushed yourself out. You did this to yourself!"

"No, no . . ." he said, panting. He sounded like he was getting tired. But then, without warning, he lunged at me, tackling me to the ground. I thrashed about, throwing punches at his eyes and nose. He dodged me every time. I tried sliding out from under him, but he was too strong and heavy. He grabbed both my hands in one of his. "You want to take her from me? You can never take her from me!" He held the trocar against my throat.

"Help us!" my mother wailed. I glanced away from Sal and saw that my mother was halfway out of the enclosure, at the end of her chain. Her whole body was shaking. Her eyes danced in their sockets. It looked like she was having a seizure. Sal followed my gaze, never lifting the trocar from my neck. "Help us!" my mother whispered.

"You shut up!" Sal yelled at her. Then, turning back to me, "I told you to stay out of my business! I told—" Sal's eyes widened. The trocar in his hand dissolved into grains of metallic sand. I could feel it slipping through his hand and onto my neck. Sal loosened his grip on me. Then, as if lifted by invisible hands, Sal's entire body rose. I scrambled up and out of the way as an unseen force slammed him hard against the wall.

The Protectors! Sal struggled against the invisible hands, screaming at me to help him.

I ran to my mother. She had stopped shaking but lay exhausted on the ground. Her eyes were barely open. "Mom?" I pulled her into a sitting position. "Mom, are you okay?"

"Yes," she whispered. "I was so afraid. . . . I called for the Protectors. I've never been so close to their world. . . ." She collapsed against me. I glanced at Sal still struggling against his invisible enemies. I didn't know how long it would last. I had to get my mother out of there. I needed something that could break her chain.

I felt along the wall, frantically looking for a tool. Suddenly, I heard something clatter to the floor, as if it had been pushed off the wall just a few feet in front of me. I raced to pick up the object—an ax. I grabbed the ax and rushed back to my mother. I began hacking away at the chain until one of the links cracked and I was able to free her.

We raced to the dumbwaiter, and I pushed my mom inside. I knew it couldn't hold us both.

"You can work the ropes and get up there, right?" I asked.

She nodded with tears in her eyes. "I'll hurry,"

she said. "I don't know how long. . . ." She glanced at Sal still pinned to the wall.

"I know," I said. "Quick, please go!"

She started pulling herself up, and I picked up the ax again.

"Let me go!" Sal yelled, thrashing his arms and legs at the unseen hands.

A moment later I heard my mother make it into the house. As I reached to grab the dumbwaiter ropes and pull it back down, something tackled me from behind. On the ground, I turned to face Sal. The Protectors had lost their grip on him. Now it was up to me. I was still clutching the ax. I tried to swing it at him from the floor, but my arm wasn't strong enough.

Sal must have been surprised by my move, because he let go of me long enough for me to get back on my feet again. But he soon regained his composure and his full strength. He grabbed my right arm, squeezing and twisting it until I dropped the ax. Quickly, I kicked it away with my feet. Sal let go of my arm and raced to retrieve the weapon. With all my strength, I leaped at him from behind, knocking him to the ground. He rolled around and started punching me. I heard a faint wailing sound somewhere above us. *Police sirens*, I thought just as everything went black.

I opened my eyes to a blur. Two figures hovered over me. Slowly they came into focus. It was my mother and Aisha.

My mother saw me blink and yelped. She came closer and smiled the warm, wide grin that I remembered from years ago. She had already regained some color in her face.

"Luke! Thank goodness!" She bent over and kissed me. "You've been out cold for three full days!"

That's when I realized I was hooked up to an IV in a hospital room.

"What happened to Sal?" I asked.

"He's alive. But the police took him away," my mother explained. "There will be a trial. He's probably going to spend the rest of his life in jail."

"I'm so glad you're okay," Aisha said. She kissed my forehead.

"Mom . . ." I could barely talk, my throat was so dry. "What happened? How did Sal capture you?"

My mother sighed deeply and began to tell her story. Sal had followed her to Mrs. McKenzie's house, but she hadn't realized he was behind her. On the way back, he'd called her on her cell phone.

"He told me he was driving behind me and that he wanted to talk. I could see him in my rearview mirror. I agreed to pull over," she explained. She had pulled over on a back road. But when she got out of the car, he attacked her. He tied her up and put her in his car. Then he pushed her car into the wall and set it ablaze with a few matches and some lighter fluid.

"He hit me in the head and knocked me out," she said, shuddering. "When I woke up, I was chained in the lower basement. But I called to my Protectors to help me, Luke. And they did. They sent you."

Suddenly, it all made sense. The weird tracks on my iPod, the song on the radio, Sheila speaking, the rash on Alice, the letters on my pancakes—they had all been messages from my mother's Protectors. The creaking in the walls at night had been Sal going up and down in the dumbwaiter! That was probably how he'd managed to get giant Frankie down to the prep room too. And, I really had heard my mother scream at night. I'd heard her chains rattling. I thought about Sal's drawing of my mother in his sketchbook. He had drawn her alive among the dead. And here she was in front of me—alive!

A few weeks later, I felt like myself again. My mother and I loaded up the back of a truck with our bare essentials—we'd sold everything in the house, including the hearse. We moved to a small house across town. It was less than a block from Aisha's. After he heard what had happened with my mother, Lincoln showed up to help us move. It looked like we would be friends again after all.

I called Bert and apologized about running out on him at the Chowder Hut that day. By the end of the call, I'd told him everything. He calls me from time to time. I'm going to meet the rest of his family when I visit him at his cabin this summer.

I've started going back to school, and my mother works as a cosmetician, doing the hair and makeup of *living* people. We've left the whole death business behind us, although my mother continues to hold séances and other rituals. I know that our Protectors are always following us, always watching us, and it doesn't creep me out. I am *protected.*

Everything's fine in Bridgewater. Really . . .

Or is it?

Look for these other titles from the
Night Fall collection.

THE CLUB

The club started innocently enough. Bored after school, Josh and his friends decided to try out an old game Sabina had found in her basement. Called "Black Magic," it promised the players good fortune at the expense of those who have wronged them. Yeah, right.

But when the club members' luck starts skyrocketing— and horror befalls their enemies—the game stops being a joke. How can they end the power they've unleashed? Answers lie in an old diary—but ending the game may be deadlier than any curse.

MESSAGES FROM BEYOND

Some guy named Ethan Davis has been texting Cassie. He seems to know all about her—but she can't place him. He's not in Bridgewater High's yearbook either. Cassie thinks one of her friends is punking her. But she can't ignore the strange coincidences—like how Ethan looks just like the guy in her nightmares.

Cassie's search for Ethan leads her to a shocking discovery—and a struggle for her life. Will Cassie be able to break free from her mysterious stalker?

SKIN

It looks like a pizza exploded on Nick Barry's face. But bad skin is the least of his problems. His bones feel like living ice. A strange rash—like scratches—seems to be some sort of ancient code. And then there's the anger . . .

Something evil is living under Nick's skin. Where did it come from? What does it want? With the help of a dead kid's diary, a nun, and a local professor, Nick slowly finds out what's wrong with him. But there's still one question that Nick must face alone: How do you destroy an evil that's *inside* you?

THAW

A July storm caused a major power outage in Bridgewater. Now a research project at the Institute for Cryogenic Experimentation has been ruined, and the thawed-out bodies of twenty-seven federal inmates are missing.

At first, Dani Kraft didn't think much of the breaking news. But after her best friend Jake disappears, a mysterious visitor connects the dots for Dani. Jake has been taken in by an infamous cult leader. To get him back, Dani must enter a dangerous, alternate reality where a defrosted cult leader is beginning to act like some kind of god.

UNTHINKABLE

Omar Phillips is Bridgewater High's favorite local teen author. His Facebook fans can't wait for his next horror story. But lately Omar's imagination has turned against him. Horrifying visions of death and destruction come over him with wide-screen intensity. The only way to stop the visions is to write them down. Until they start coming true . . .

Enter Sophie Minax, the mysterious Goth girl who's been following Omar at school. "I'm one of you," Sophie says. She tells Omar how to end the visions—but the only thing worse than Sophie's cure may be what happens if he ignores it.